Crocs at Work...

For Judy Brown: Her work was her play. — R.H.

For Mason, Abby, Jayden and Itai, youngest members of my
excellent extended family: These silly Crocs are for YOU! — R.M.

Published by Tradewind Books in Canada and the UK in 2015
Text copyright © 2015 Robert Heidbreder • Illustrations copyright © 2015 Rae Maté

The publisher wishes to thank the editor, Tiffany Stone, for her glorious contribution to this book.
The publisher also wishes to thank Olga Lenczewska and Ayushi Nayak for their editorial assistance with this book.

Art direction by Carol Frank • Book design by Elisa Gutiérrez • The text of this book is set in Providence-Sans and Carnation.

10   9   8   7   6   5   4   3   2   1

. . . .

LIBRARY AND ARCHIVES CANADA CATALOGUING IN PUBLICATION

Heidbreder, Robert, author
     Crocs at work / Robert Heidbreder ; illustrated by Rae Maté.

(Crocodiles say, crocodiles play)
ISBN 978-1-926890-04-3 (bound)

I. Maté, Rae, 1948-, illustrator II. Title.

PS8565.E42C78 2015   jC813'.54   C2015-903077-3

. . . .

Printed and bound
in Korea on ancient
forest-friendly paper.

The publisher thanks the Government of Canada and Canadian Heritage for their
financial support through the Canada Council for the Arts, the Canada Book Fund and
Livres Canada Books. The publisher also thanks the Government of the Province
of British Columbia for the financial support it has given through the Book
Publishing Tax Credit program and the British Columbia Arts Council.

 Canada Council   Conseil des Arts
for the Arts   du Canada

 BRITISH
COLUMBIA
ARTS COUNCIL

Robert Heidbreder and Rae Maté

Crocs at Work...

TRADEWIND · BOOKS

VANCOUVER · LONDON

Bus driver Crocs are safety-proud:
"We never speed! No risks allowed!
No sudden stops! All signs obeyed!
SAFETY FIRST! is our crusade."
So, to stick to every rule . . .

As postal carriers supreme,
in weather sunny or extreme,
Crocs guarantee they'll never fail,
delivering each piece of mail.
And, to make their work more fun . . .

Crocs hide the mail

from everyone!

Croc docs and nurses rank first-rate.
All ills they make evaporate.
They never prod. They never poke.
NO TEARS ALLOWED! for small Croc folk.
"We'll fix your owies," they declare . . .

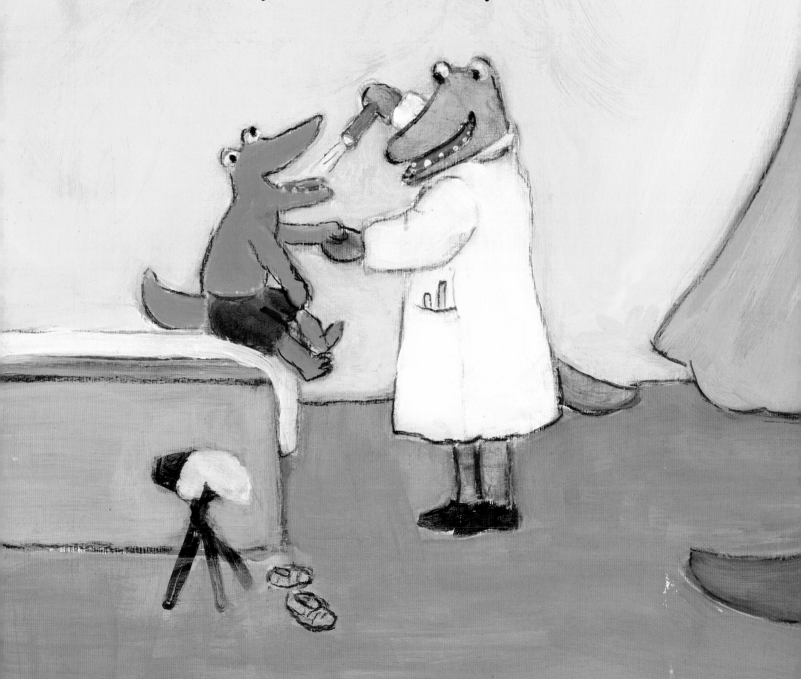

As gourmet cooks, Crocs work with speed.
They heed each diner's every need,
concocting any scrumptious dish
to suit a diner's wildest wish.
But, to ensure the fare tastes right . . .

House-painting Crocs are in demand
for tasteful eye and skillful hand.
They feel each house should stand apart—
a chic, unique Croc work of art—
subtle, tranquil, calm and quaint . . .

So every house
they splatter-paint!

In florist shops, all Crocs are pros,
creating feasts for eyes and nose.
They pick and choose the freshest flowers,
arrange bouquets for hours and hours.
When each bouquet's the sweetest treat . . .

As teachers, Crocs are truly great.
Ideal skills they demonstrate.
They know what small Crocs need to learn.
They're never angry, cross or stern.
The way they teach is quite sublime.
Croc teachers say . . .